Sonship Childrens Books Vol. 1

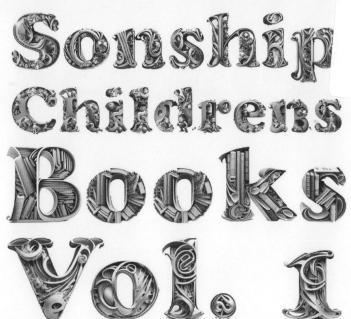

WRITTEN AND CREATED BY
SONSHIP CHILDREN'S BOOKS

Dedicated To "Pops"
2023

In the beginning, when the world was new,
God created life and a sky so blue.

God made the plants, the stars, and the seas,
And filled the world with **buzzing bees.**

With love and care, He thought it through,
And then He made just two to **debut**.

Two genders He created, each unique,
Both strong and gentle, bold and
meek

God made a boy and He made a girl,
Each a treasure, a beautiful *pearl.*

Exploring the world in their own special way.

They'd balance each other, like two sides of a scale,
Creating harmony with love that

Prevails

I Am A Spirit

WRITTEN AND CREATED BY
SONSHIP CHILDREN'S BOOKS

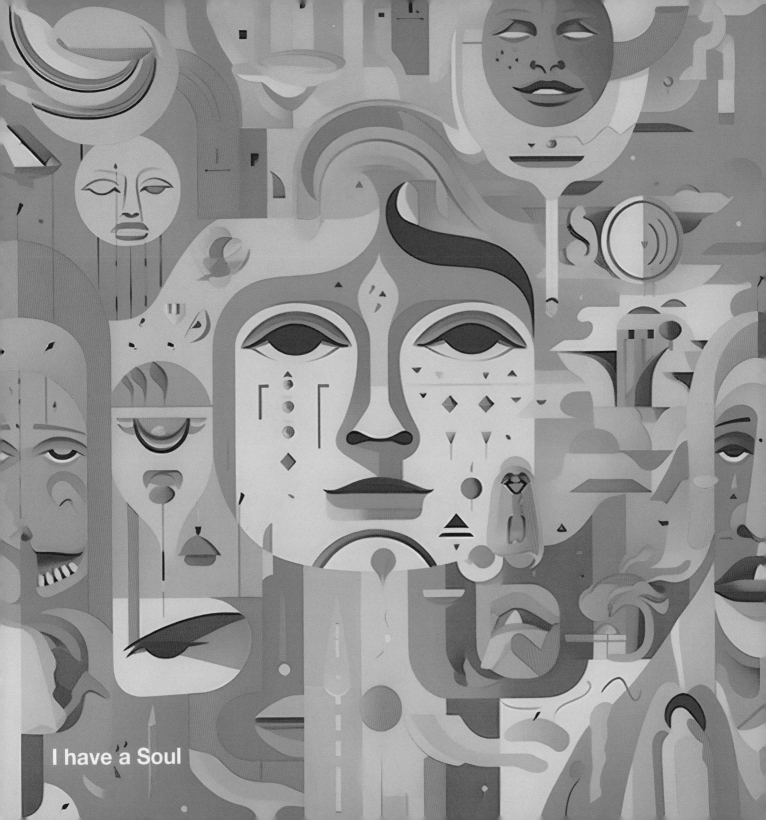

I have a Soul

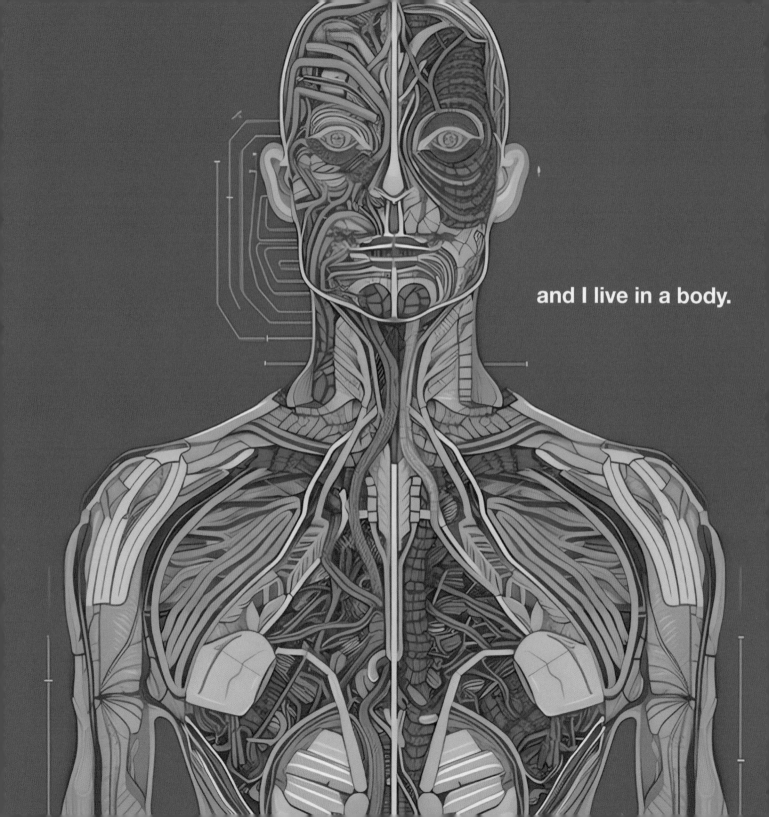

and I live in a body.

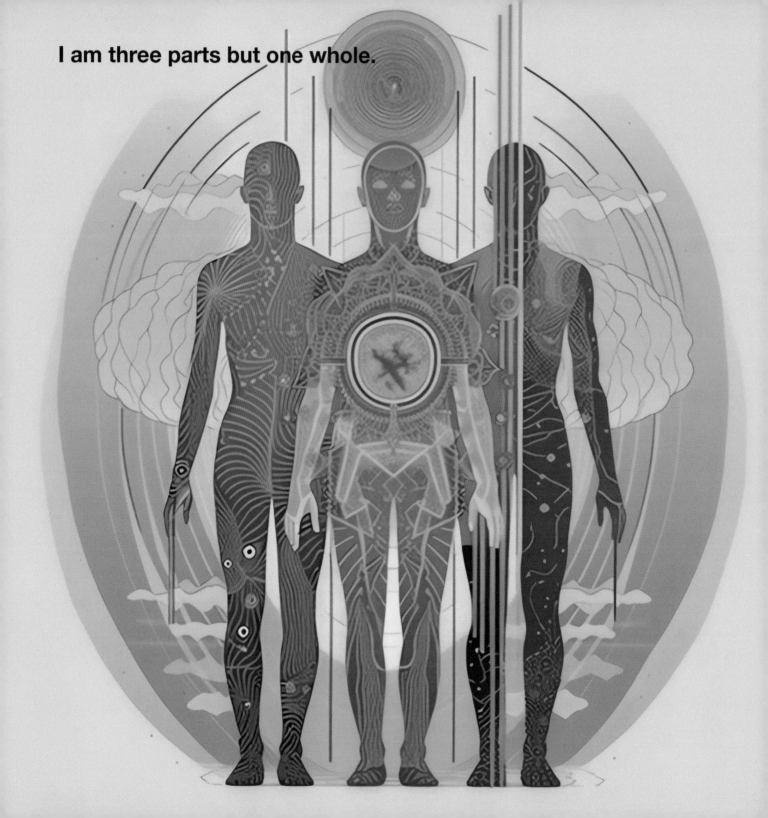

Like God, Jesus, and Holy Spirit are 3 in 1.

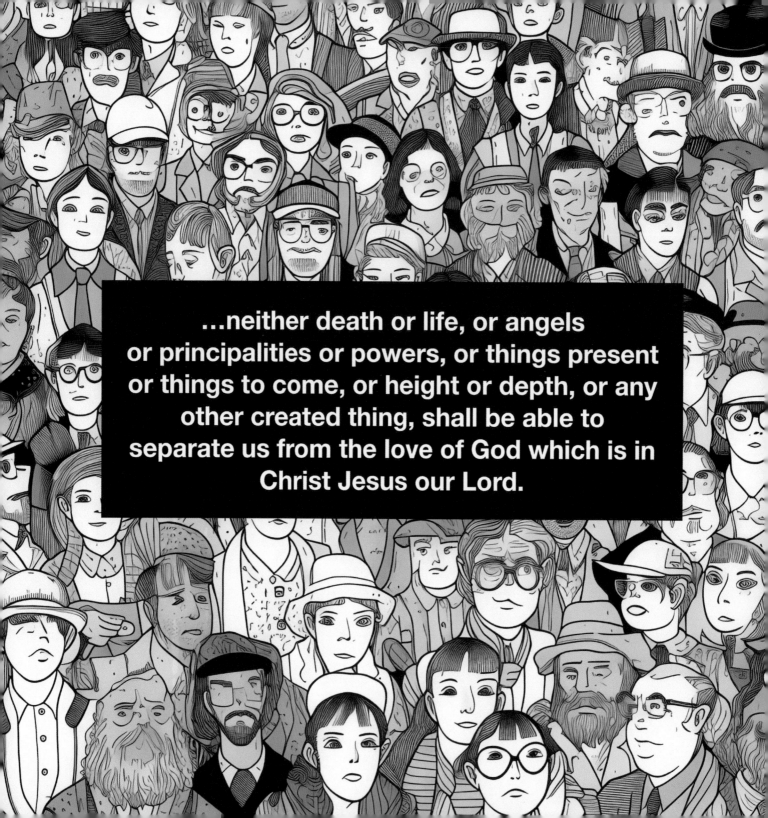

...neither death or life, or angels or principalities or powers, or things present or things to come, or height or depth, or any other created thing, shall be able to separate us from the love of God which is in Christ Jesus our Lord.

Little Lamb

WRITTEN AND ILLUSTRATED BY
SONSHIP CHILDREN'S BOOKS

On a hillside green and bright,
A shepherd watched his sheep with delight.

But one little sheep had got away,

And the shepherd knew he couldn't stay.

To search for the lost sheep before the day was done.

He looked high and low, left and right,

Until he found it, what a sight!

God's love is like the shepherd's grace,

Always seeking us in every place.

The Honest

Quokka

WRITTEN AND ILLUSTRATED BY
SONSHIP CHILDREN'S BOOKS

This is a young quokka named Sammy.
Sammy loves to play with his friends and

explore the beautiful island
where they live.

One day, Sammy found a rock he liked on the ground.

Sammy was so excited to show his friends.

His friends asked where he got the rock.
Sammy wanted to impress his friends.

so he told them he found it on the beach.

But then Sammy started feeling guilty.
He didn't want to lie to his friends.

So he told them the truth, that he actually found the rock in his mom's garden.

From that day on Sammy knew that the truth is always more impressive than a lie.

FEARLESS FUTURE

WRITTEN AND ILLUSTRATED BY
SUNSHIP CHILDREN'S BOOKS

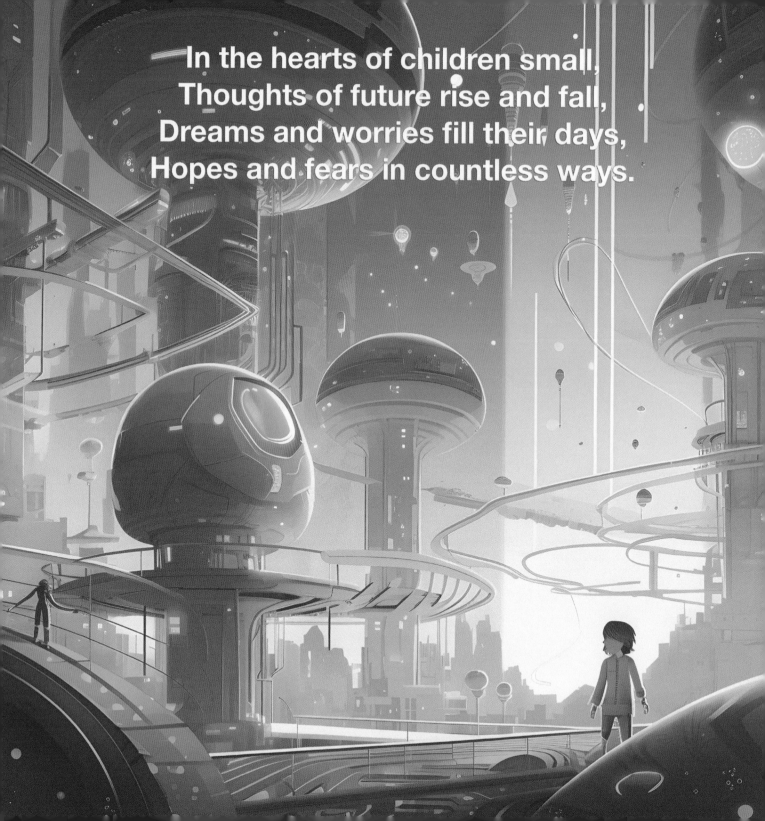

In the hearts of children small,
Thoughts of future rise and fall,
Dreams and worries fill their days,
Hopes and fears in countless ways.

But within you,
Lies a gift, His perfect love,
A love that's strong, so vast and deep,
Holding them when your awake or asleep.

Fear not the future, children dear,
For God's great love is always near,
He whispers softly in your ear,
His perfect love casts out all fear.

Through twists and turns, come what may,
Jesus loving guidance lights the way,
The future may be unknown, it's true,
But in Jesus love, there's peace for you.

Young hearts, be strong, be brave, be free,
In God's love, find your destiny,
The future's like an open door,
His love will guide you evermore.

When doubt or worry clouds your way,
Remember His love, and do not sway,
For in His arms, you'll find your place,
Where perfect love and hope embrace.

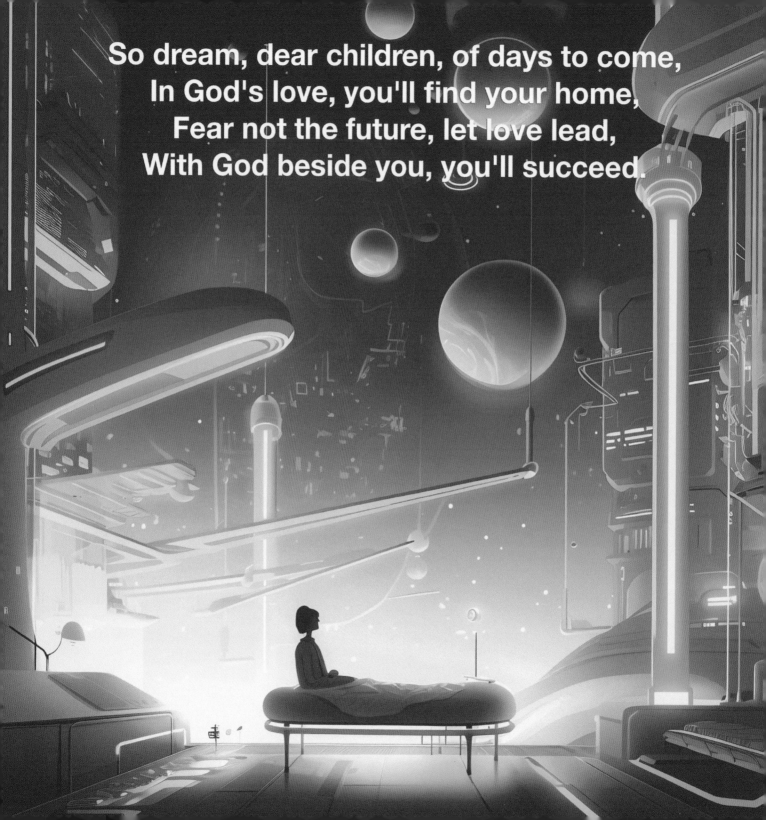

So dream, dear children, of days to come,
In God's love, you'll find your home,
Fear not the future, let love lead,
With God beside you, you'll succeed.

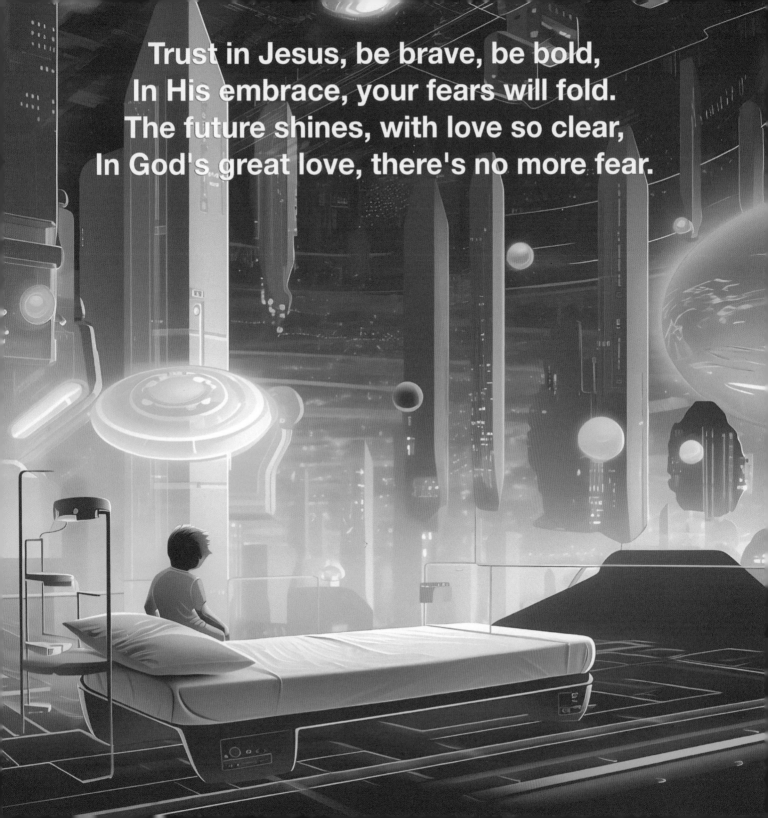

Trust in Jesus, be brave, be bold,
In His embrace, your fears will fold.
The future shines, with love so clear,
In God's great love, there's no more fear.

A Little Bird

WRITTEN AND CREATED BY
SONSHIP CHILDREN'S BOOKS

Once upon a time, there was a little bird,
Who chirped and sang, never saying a word,
He woke up each morning with the rising sun,
And flew all day, having so much fun.

He never worried about what he would eat,

Or where he would sleep,

or the ground beneath his feet,

For he knew that his Heavenly Father above,
Would take care of him with His unfailing love.

"Look at the birds;

they do not
sow or reap,

Can any one of you
by worrying
add a single hour to
your life?"

Jesus Loves
TO DANCE

WRITTEN AND CREATED BY
SONSHIP CHILDREN'S BOOKS

There once was a girl who loved to dance,
She twirled and spun at every chance.

In school, her room, and the family too,
She'd dance and prance the whole day through.

With music in her heart and feet,
She'd tap and shimmy to the beat,

But little did
they know,
you see,
That God
was dancing
just like she,

The Lord of the dance,
so light and free,
Guiding her steps so
effortlessly.

For she knows that in every dance, God's love and grace is her true stance,

And in His love, she'll always be, The happiest dancer, wild and free.

So let us dance, with wild and carefree bliss,
In this divine waltz of love and peace,
For with every step, we're embraced by grace,
Guided by the Lord's divine embrace.

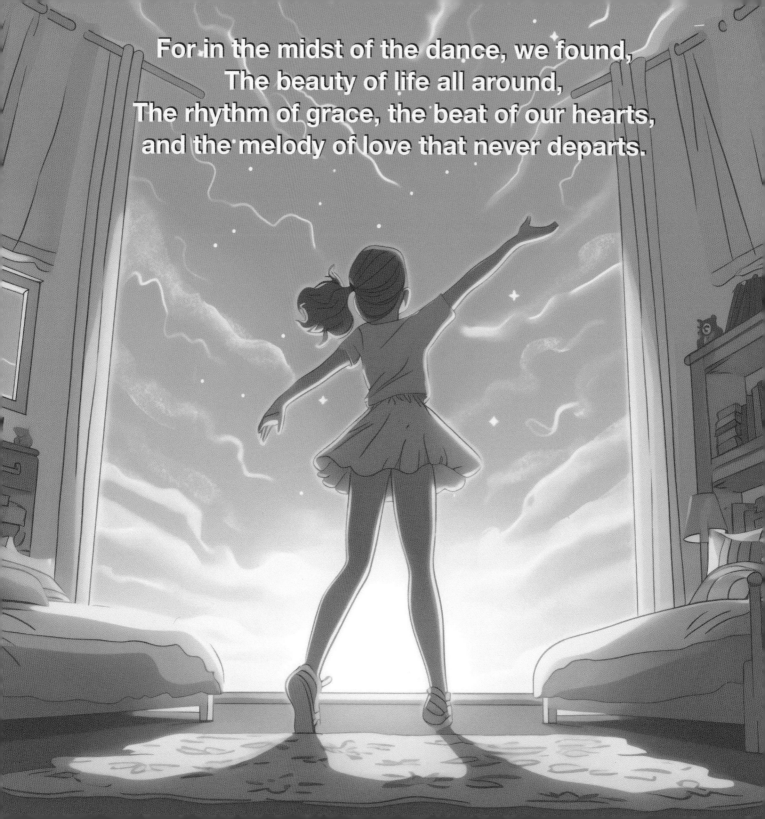

Timmy & The Frog

WRITTEN AND CREATED BY
SONSHIP CHILDREN'S BOOKS

Once upon a summer's day,
By the pond where froggies play,
Billy met a frog named Fred,
Whose words of wisdom soon he'd spread.

Fred the frog, with voice so wise,
Taught young Billy to recognize,

When Holy Spirit speaks inside,
To help him choose, to be his guide.

"Listen close," Fred said with cheer,
"Let the Spirit guide you, dear.
In this world of choices wide,
He will be your faithful guide."

Billy nodded, his eyes so wide,
Ready to let the Spirit guide,

With each hop, young Billy knew,
The Holy Spirit would guide him through,

Choices big and choices small,
Always listen to the Spirit's call.

TALK TO JESUS

WRITTEN AND CREATED BY
SONSHIP CHILDREN'S BOOKS

On the playground,

or under a tree,

When you wake up and the sun is shining,

Remember you're a son of God, that's so exciting!

It means you are special

and loved every day

And Jesus is always one with you

and never far away

Sometimes life can be tough

But don't worry

Jesus is always there to lend a helping hand.

If you make a mistake

and turn your frown upside down

So when you're feeling happy

or a little sad,

Rise Up My son Try Again

Once upon a time in a room full of grace,
Lived a little girl who loved to embrace,
The wonderful world of ballet dance,
In her cozy bedroom, she'd twirl and prance.

She practiced her pliés, arabesques, and leaps,
And in her heart, the Son of God she'd keep,
For He was the one who made her strong,
In His loving arms, she'd forever belong.

One day as she danced, she tripped and fell,
But a gentle voice whispered, "All is well,
Rise up, my son, and try again,
For I am with you, every step, my friend."

With newfound strength and courage in her soul,
The little dancer continued to strive for her goal,
For she knew she was loved, and never alone,
As a son of God, she had found her true home.

As the days went by, her dancing grew bright,
Her leaps and turns soared with heavenly light,
For the love of God had shown her the way,
To rise after falling and dance every day.

Always A Good Chat

In a little town not far away,

A little child
awakes for the day.

Brushing their
teeth with
a smile so wide

**Ready to explore
the world outside.**

In their backyard

They
pretended to
be in a forest
full of trees

And stumble upon a sight that was hard to believe

There, in a
meadow,
bathed in
light,

Stood their friend Jesus, shining bright.

**They sat
and talked
about love,
kindness,
and peace**

And how to make sadness and anger cease.

Jesus told
the child
that in their
heart,

love for
others is
where
they
should
always
start.

For loving
your
neighbor,
your
family,
your
friend,

Printed in Great Britain
by Amazon

22002643R00075